Anyone *and* *You*

Jack Whitney

To all my spooky bitches that are
tired of the damn summer heat
and the unrelenting sweat,
and just want to feel that cool breeze of
autumn brush over their skin and all the
fall things that come with it.

This one is for you.

Anyone And You

is an autumn erotica novella.

I am putting a warning on this because it does feature
graphic sex and a heavy amount of autumn and fall vibes
that could potentially make you want to head out to the
local fall festival to get finger fucked on the teacups and
have a nice warm apple cider drink after.

If you don't get nauseous, that is.
Do not recommend if you get nauseous.
Actually, this act would be illegal (don't get caught).

The following are the sexual acts to be aware of:
Public play, choking, and toys

Please don't go looking for some overly dramatic plot.
There isn't one.

Enjoy the next eighty pages of fun.

Chapter One
Des

Have you ever had a date that completely swept you off your feet and had you feeling butterflies for days after—checking your phone for the next cute text, hoping they ask you out again?

Yeah, me either.

Maybe that's why I'd always loved blind dates instead of the usual online dating trend. Expectations? A nice face and a good fuck at the end of the night would do—preferably in some public place so I never had to worry about the awkward moments of kicking him out, having to fake it to get him to finish, or, on the rare occasion, the silent car ride to his apartment.

I bristled at that thought. I'd rather get caught and flash someone a view of my ass before enduring those situations.

Or maybe that's just me.

The cool autumn breeze swept around me as I walked through the park to my blind date that night. I was a little antsy about this one. Mutual friends set it up—an entire night at the local Equinox Festival, including all the cutesy things like hay bales and carnival rides.

I was so fucking excited. Regardless of who it was I was meeting, I knew I would have fun. And if he was dull, I could always leave him and have plenty to do on my own. Eat a funnel cake. Play a few games. Talk to the local vendors and see what they make. Get lost in the Hall of Mirrors. Finish myself off on the Ferris wheel or the spinning tea cups.

You know, the usual things one does at a Fall Festival. That thrill made me smile as I continued walking up the hill to the bench where I was supposed to meet my date. I had to walk on my toes, careful not to trip with my thick-heeled boots sinking into the grass. I could already hear the live music playing on the stage, the laughter and screams from the carnival rides strumming over the air. The breeze carried the smells of the festival on it—sweet cinnamon, apples, freshly stirred dirt, and a bite of clean chill.

Autumn.

It smelled like the perfect autumn candle, and I wanted to bottle it up and bring it back to my apartment to burn year-round.

As I reached the top of the hill, I looked around the other benches for any sign of my date. I was told he'd bring a sunflower, and I was to wear a grey sweater and boots. But that was all the information I'd been given besides my friends' approval of him.

All the people on the benches were families, couples, and a few children—no single man carrying a sunflower. I chose a bench, took my phone out, and sat to wait on him. I was a few minutes early, about five to be exact, so I pulled up the camera on my phone and decided to take a few pictures while I waited.

Golden hour in autumn was a different breed than golden hour any other time of the year. The hour before sunset—the autumn sun had a way of hitting the trees and cascading light that practically melted yellows, golds, and purples into the air. It was my favorite time of the year as a photographer. As I composed a photo of a couple under a changing sugar maple tree, I made a note to come back the next night with my Sony camera.

I took a few photos of the trees, of a leaf on the bench beside me, and one of me waiting—just my legs in view, the maple tree, the leaf, and the hill in the background. As I looked through them, posting the one of me waiting on social media, I realized I had completely missed that I'd also gotten my mystery man in the photo's background.

My gaze shot up as I closed the phone, and my heart skipped in the usual rushing way it did upon finding out who I was meeting on a blind date.

My jaw nearly dropped as I realized who it was—that I knew him.

No. Fucking. Way.

I almost laughed at the situation I was in, at who was carrying a sunflower and trudging over the grass like he was leaving ash in his wake.

His name was Axel Connors, and he lived in the apartment across from me.

Axel.

Of course, his name couldn't have been Josh, Corey, or John. It had to be Axel. And, of course, he had to look like he'd just walked out of the Colorado wilderness at all times. He had dark chestnut hair, a beard that wrapped over his strong jaw, and a neck that rivaled Gaston. On more than one occasion, I had teased him in the hall and asked if he could snap a belt with that neck. He usually responded with a grunt, but the last time... the last time I'd asked, he'd told me that he had much better uses for a belt. He'd looked me over in a way that made my thighs squeeze but had shut the door behind him before I could ask more.

He was wearing the exact same navy, grey, and white flannel he always wore with dark, snug-fitting jeans, grey boots, and the same damn beanie that... Dammit, he did look sexy in that beanie.

He was sexy all the time, but that beanie… it did something to me. I loved how the flannel shirt hugged his biceps and broad shoulders, and how it was opened the top few buttons. And how he had the sleeves rolled up to his elbows and showcased the veins in his forearms… *sweet fuck.*

Ever since he moved into the apartment across the hall a year ago, I'd always had a crush on Axel. He was tall, sexy, bearded, muscled, mysterious. Muscled, not necessarily in the completely trim way you'd see so many actors depriving themselves to fit into an action role for a movie. No, Axel was a beast. A solid tree built for climbing.

He was a man of few words, angry at the world, and an asshole when he wanted to be. I wasn't even sure I'd ever seen him smile.

And yet, there he was. Walking across the field with a sunflower in his hand, the autumn sun bouncing off his alabaster skin, creating shadows in every crease of his muscles, looking as mad as ever—

But willingly on a blind date.

I wondered if this was my chance to crack that exterior of his. I wondered what he was hiding, if I could actually get him to smile, just once.

The challenge became my goal for the evening. Even if this date was a total flop, and I ended up in worse shape over him than I was already in, I would get him to smile.

Chapter Two
Axel

I hadn't been on an actual date in months.

My fucking friends think they're slick, setting me up like this. But I'd said yes simply to get them to shut up. I'd even picked up this sunflower on the way like they'd asked—a five-minute detour that made me late, and I hated being late.

I told myself if the woman I was meeting wasn't there by the time I got there, I would leave, tell my friends she hadn't shown, and maybe go inside the carnival to get a stiff drink.

I looked up the hill then to see if I saw my date. She was supposed to be wearing a grey sweater and boots, and I half hoped she would be a no-show or maybe see me and run away.

As I scanned the benches, I noted the families and the couples, and then I spotted someone familiar. Someone I definitely didn't want to run into tonight, *especially* not tonight —

Fuck. Maybe she hadn't seen me.
I looked away quickly and started to zag the other way to the sidewalk, but—

My stomach dropped, and I halted as I realized *she* was wearing a grey sweater. *She* was wearing boots, and she was staring at me like she knew exactly why I was there.

Not her.

Anyone but her.

Her name was Desiree Allen, Des for short, and she lived across the hall from me.

"Axel Connors," she called out to me.

Fucking hell. I wasn't sure what I had prepared myself for, but I knew I hadn't prepared myself for her. Her, I couldn't avoid. Her, I couldn't just run away from and think I'd never see her again. Her, I didn't know what I would do if this date went badly.

But dammit, she was gorgeous.

She'd recently dyed her hair a dark purple-burgundy—mulberry, or so she'd told me when I'd seen her in the hallway—for the fall season. Her long layered hair fell in waves around her face. The color accentuated her golden skin and dark brows, the dark eye-makeup she'd chosen for tonight, and the pink lipstick.

I'd tried to keep my distance from her over the last year. She was so damn chipper, and that smile... that smile, her laugh... they drove me fucking insane.

My mouth dried at the sight of her watching me come up the hill, that smile on her face as she realized it was me she was waiting on. Her almond-tipped nails strummed once on her cheek as she held her face in her hand, and her doe eyes danced in amusement.

I threw the sunflower over my shoulder and turned around.

"Oh no—" She stood off the bench and started toward me, and I couldn't help stopping my exit to look her over in that black short skirt, the pantyhose covering her thick thighs, and the black boots that came all the way up over her knees. The dark grey sweater fell over one of her shoulders, exposing her collar, bra strap, and the pillow of her full breast. I stiffened at how sexy she looked and tried not to let it show on my face.

Fuck. There was no getting out of this.

I was doomed.

"You're not getting out of this date," she said, laughter in her tone. "Hi, Axel."

A low grunt of frustration sounded in my throat. "Des," I replied, looking her over again. "Did you know?" I asked, getting suspicious by the way she didn't seem surprised.

She laughed. "Fuck, no," she said. "I'm as baffled by this as you. But I think…" Her gaze darted over me, taking in every inch of my body and almost making me shift and stand up straighter. But her long lashes lifted, hitting her eyelids, and she bit her lip.

I really wished she wouldn't do that.

"This will be so much fun," she finally said.

"This is a bad idea."

But she wrapped her arm into mine and tugged me forward. "Oh, sunshine… I think it's a perfect idea," she said, smiling up at me. My stomach knotted at that smile, at the way she was looking at me. The warmth of her arm wrapped into mine.

A fucking terrible idea.

"Come on," she said. "A friend told me they have apple cider moonshine in here somewhere. I'll buy us a couple of shots to get us started."

Chapter Three
Des

As we entered the festival, a few kids ran past us through the stacked hay bales and iron archway. I kept sneaking glances at Axel, feeling how stiff he was at my side. He didn't say anything as I doted on a few vendors' homemade products and even purchased a few candles and a t-shirt. Axel stood off to the side to wait on me, apparently judging every purchase I made—his arms crossed, eyes downcast and slightly squinted, jaw taut.

"What?" I asked.

"Nothing," he said. "By the way your apartment smells, I thought you'd had enough candles."

"No such thing," I replied, falling into step at his side. "You know, I actually find it hard to believe the apartment complex we stay in fits your rugged aesthetic," I teased. "Shouldn't you be in the woods? Far, far away, chopping trees or something more... rustic?" I looked him up and down. The unkept beard, the muscles straining against his old flannel he'd obviously been wearing for years now.

That bristle I'd come to love pulling out of him flashed in his hazel green eyes, so much more vibrant here against the sunset, and I smiled at the sight of it.

"You're cute when you glare like that," I said. I spotted the sign for the drinks and jerked my chin toward it.

"Drink?"

"Please," he grunted.

The whiskey truck wasn't as packed as I expected, and we were through the line in minutes. Two shots each in hand, I raised my first one to his.

"To a night of breaking through that exterior of yours," I said.

Axel squinted at me. "What?"

"Nothing," I said, deciding to keep it to myself. "Cheers," I chose instead.

His plastic cup touched mine, and we both choked back the burning liquid in one gulp. I shook my head at the sting, making a noise, and then watched as Axel's expression barely moved. He grabbed the second shot we'd ordered and downed it as well.

A dribble of liquid escaped and dripped down his beard, the liquid coating his lips, and I suddenly wondered what his mouth would look like with what he could do to me covering his lips. How that beard would have felt on my thighs, tickling my pussy…

Wishful thinking, Des, I thought to myself.

I'd pleasured myself to the thought of him between my thighs more times than I could count but never loud enough for him to hear. Maybe once he left me for the night, I'd use that image to get off. Maybe let myself moan his name a little louder in the hopes he heard me through the walls and realized what he was missing out on.

"So," I said, breaking out of my daze. "What do you want to do first?" I sipped the second shot as I let him think it over. "Games? Carnival rides? Food? Haunted house?"

"No haunted houses," he said.

I bit my lip to keep from smiling. "Not scared, are you?"

"I don't like things jumping out at me," he replied. "Unless you'd like tonight to end with me in handcuffs in the back of a squad car."

"Well, maybe not in the back of a squad car, but the thought of you in handcuffs does intrigue me," I said before downing the rest of my drink and pushing off the rail we'd paused to stand beside.

"Fucking hell, Des," he grunted. "Someone should *really* stuff that smart mouth of yours," he added, and I smirked at him over my shoulder as I turned.

"Volunteering?" I asked, giving him a once over, my eyes lingering on his snug-fitting jeans for a moment longer than I should have.

His gaze caught mine, my smile growing wider upon seeing the slight ease in that frustrating shell of his. Two shots of alcohol. Was that the secret?

I laughed as I started forward, but he grabbed my arm before I could get a step away. I was thrust off balance and back into his embrace, flush against that broad chest, my arms now trapped between our bodies as his other hand enclosed around my waist.

This was too close for the thoughts spinning in my mind, for all the images I couldn't help but see. I wondered if he could see the need and lust in my eyes there.

We were so close that I could feel the breeze of his breath on my lips.

And for whatever reason, he didn't let me go.

"If I ever decide to do that," he began, his voice gruffer than usual. "You'll wish you'd chosen your desires more carefully."

"You're not the first man to threaten me with a good time, Axel," I said, ignoring the loud thumping of my heart.

"No," he agreed. "But I'd be the last one you remember."

He released me abruptly, and I staggered off balance, catching an amused glint in his eyes. But it was gone within the next second, and I was left contemplating whether or not

I'd imagined it.

I straightened my sweater and choked my desire down into the smallest corner of my being before saying, "Who knew such a crab could have a dirty little mouth like that?"

Something of a chuckle sounded from him as he shook his head. Barely a laugh, but something more than what I'd ever heard from him, though a lasting smile didn't accompany it.

"Games," he said. "Let's see how the princess plays."

Chapter Four

Des

Princess.

He'd called me that name a few times before, after I'd called him sunshine once. But right then, I wasn't sure I cared that he meant it condescendingly. It suddenly sounded so cocky on his tongue, as if he knew what that word might do to me.

Asshole.

I caught up with him in a few strides and tucked my arm into his once more. We passed the other vendors, the food trucks, and the stage where bands were already playing. There was a popular local band poised to play at 9pm that night and were slated until the fireworks began later. I wondered if their music was what Axel was into, though from what I'd heard coming out of his apartment, he was usually into rock music.

Rows of fluorescent lights caught my gaze ahead, along with lines and lines of gaming booths—everything from ring toss to the one with the fish bowls. Axel paused at my side and looked around.

"Which one?" he asked.

"I'm very tempted to watch you hit that bell—" I said, only half teasing. Watching him strike the target with that giant mallet and break the bell at the top would be the highlight of my night.

Axel eyed me sideways, and I couldn't tell if he was amused or not. "You want the big bear, don't you?" he asked, jerking his chin to the largest teddy bear I'd ever seen hanging over the game's bell.

"Maybe later," I said before looking around. "For now, let's do ring toss," I decided. "I'm decent at that one."

The attendant at the ring toss booth looked the most bored out of all the attendants there. He was lazily calling attention to the game, twirling a few rings on his fingers as he did, and when we approached, he gave us a judgemental once over.

"Ten rings for the lady, ten rings for the lady," he said as I took out a few dollars to give him.

Axel stood at my back and watched over my shoulder. I hadn't played the game in a few years, but the competitor in me was determined to win this.

"Which prize are you looking to win?" Axel asked me.

I glanced up at the stuffed animals hanging from the top of the tent. "The blue raccoon," I said.

"Three games, lady," the attendant said. "You'll need to win three games."

"That's three times the cost of that stuffed animal," Axel said.

"Hey, I don't make the rules, friend—Step right up, step right up—"

Axel blew out a breath and shook his head. I laughed. "You hate these games, don't you?"

He shifted his feet and hugged his arms to his chest, obviously irritated by the attendant. "Not when they're fair," he said. "Make sure you win, princess."

I settled into my stance and then let the rings fly one by one. Each ring hit its target, and when I won the first round, I clapped excitedly and started to reach for a few dollars more for the next game.

"I got it," Axel said as he stopped me. He fleshed out money to the attendant, practically shoving it in his hand. "Two games," Axel told him.

"Big spender, big spender," the attendant called out. "Alright. Two more games for the pretty little lady—" He placed the rings in a bucket and handed it to me.

Axel stepped up behind me, his shoulder against my back. His hand grazed the top of my hip, and I swallowed at his proximity.

"Sink them before I punch this idiot for robbing you," he said.

"You can't expect me to concentrate with you so close, Axel," I managed, and I wasn't exaggerating.

A scoff left him, and he settled at my side. "Better?" he asked. The glint of amusement was back, and I felt a jagged breath leave me at the sight of it.

"For now," I said. I readied my stance again and once more tossed the rings. Every time I landed one, Axel made a grunt of approval, and I could see him glaring at the attendant from the corner of my eye. When I had five rings left, he uncrossed his arms and braced his palms onto the barrier.

"Let's go, princess," he said, his gruff way of cheering me on.

"Five to go—can she do it? Let's see, folks—"

Axel's grip tightened on the wood at the sound of the attendant's voice, but I tried to ignore it and land the last few.

One—two—three— We had a few people watching now. Axel gave me a high-five; his gruff voice and small celebration must have caught people's attention. I felt my face light up at him actually getting into this, though I knew it was to spite the ever-watchful attendant.

"Two more," he said, getting antsy at my side. "You got this."

My stomach knotted at his assurance, and I bit my bottom lip in concentration.

One in.

Axel clapped his hands twice, shifting from foot to foot. "Come on, princess," he said under his breath.

I aimed and let the ring go. It landed on one in the middle and circled the rim of the glass, making both of us clench our fists as we waited on it to fall one way or the other. I grabbed Axel's arm when it started to sink. I had won. I had—

The attendant stuck his poker into the sea of glasses and began gathering the rings.

"Too bad, too bad," he said. "Better luck in the next round for that one. Pick a prize from the front row, little lady."

"What—" I couldn't believe it. Fucking—

"I believe the lady won," Axel said, stepping up in front of me.

"Sorry, friend," the attendant said. "Last one didn't fall. Too close. How about one more round? Five out of ten, and she wins the raccoon."

Axel lunged across the barrier. Rings flew off the poker as Axel grabbed the attendant by the collar and yanked him forward. My heart jumped into my throat at the rage in Axel's eyes, the white of his knuckles on the attendant's shirt.

"The way I see it, *friend*, is that her last ring sank, and she won," Axel practically snarled. "Give her the fucking raccoon before I come over this barrier."

Shit.

I was ready to pin him against any wall I could find and beg him to fuck me until I lost control and forgot my name.

"Okay, okay," the attendant said, his hands up. "Let me down."

I realized then that Axel had picked him up off the ground. He slowly let the man down, the man's shirt creased from the fist Axel had taken of it. Axel released him and gave the man two pats on his cheek.

"The fluffy one," Axel said as I wrapped my hand around his arm.

"Axel, you don't—"

"No one takes your smile away," he said upon meeting my eyes.

I didn't know what to say, didn't know how to look away. He *meant* it. My hand tightened around his forearm, the only way I knew how to respond.

The attendant hesitantly reached for the stuffed animal and took it down from the rafters. Axel's gaze tore from mine, and he snatched the raccoon from the attendant's grasp.

"That's better," Axel muttered. He gave me the raccoon, and I cuddled it close to me as we turned. Onlookers cat-called and moved out of our way, a few women leering at Axel as we passed, but he didn't seem to notice.

It was only when we'd gotten out of earshot that I found my voice again.

"You didn't have to do that," I said.

Axel paused to face me. "I did," he said. "The look on your face when he did that... I couldn't stand to see it. And I hate cheats." He glared back over his shoulder at the still baffled attendant. "I hate people like that taking advantage of people. Carnivals are always crawling with crooks looking to make a buck."

I reached out and reassuringly rubbed his arm. "Such a cynic," I mocked, trying to ease his mood. "There's more to festivals than cheats and thieves. Look at all these happy people. Don't you hear the laughter?"

A heavy sigh left him. He took his beanie off and ran a hand through his dark hair before shaking his head. "I scared you," he said as he met my eyes.

I balked slightly. "What—by threatening that idiot for

being a swindler? No," I reassured him. I took the beanie from his hands and put it back on his head, catching the swallow and dilated gaze he was looking at me with. "It was pretty hot."

The corner of his lips flinched like he might smile, but for the thousandth time, it seemed I'd imagined it.

But I was determined.

"Come on," I said, slipping my arm into his again. "I think I've had enough of the games. Time for rides—we'll start slow," I said with a wink.

"Is there any other way?" he said, taking me by surprise.

I glanced sideways at him. "Not if you want to truly enjoy it."

There was desire in his eyes, and I hoped he couldn't feel the way my heart was racing right then.

Chapter Five
Axel

She would be the death of me.

The look on her face when that cheat tried to keep her from winning... I thought I'd lose my mind. But the way she just looked at me, the way I felt when she was so excited about that damn game...

I was in deep shit.

I paid for the ride tickets at the booth, brushing her off when she offered to pay instead.

"Six tickets each," I said as I held them up to her. "Choose wisely."

That smile melted me to my knees as she took her six from my hand. "Teacups," she said.

My entire face furrowed at the word, and I glanced behind her toward the teacups ride. "Isn't that for kids?"

"Not entirely," she said before taking my hand. "You don't get motion sick, do you?"

I shook my head. "Never. You?"

"The adrenaline usually keeps it at bay," she answered. "Come on."

I let her pull me into that ride, where quite a few kids and their parents were also on it. Once we were seated, she laughed at the expression on my face.

"Oh, come on, grumpy face," she said. "Let it go. Have a

little fun."

She made me want to.

Fuck.

The ride began, and we both placed our hands on the wheel. She looked around at the others, at how slow they were spinning, and a wicked glint rose in her eyes.

"Faster than everyone else," she said. "So fast we throw up."

"Never going to happen," I replied.

"Then I guess we can go pretty damn fast," she said. "Start spinning, sunshine."

It became a game quicker than I realized it would. Within seconds, we were trying to outdo each other, fixated on somehow getting that cup to spin so fast that we would be thrown off of it.

Her laugh filled my ears, and for the first time in a long time, I felt my walls crumbling down. I wanted to laugh too. I wanted to let go, throw my head back, and be as in the moment as she was.

She looked so damn gorgeous, more so than usual. The delight on her face, her eyes scrunched and closed, how wild her hair flew around with the wind. I wished I could have grabbed my phone to take a picture of it.

However, the thought left my mind when I could no longer contain myself. The wind whipped my face so fast that it hurt, but her laugh was contagious. Her happiness poured through me, and I felt it coming from deep within me before I could stop it.

The next thing I knew, I was laughing with her.

I hadn't laughed like that in over a year. *She* had pulled that out of me. She had gotten something from me that no one had been able to in so long.

My heart swelled as our laughter turned to soft chuckles, and as our eyes met, we both realized what had happened. She scooted closer to me, and I kept spinning the wheel, coming down from the high she'd just put me on. And when she was directly at my side, she pressed her hand to my cheek.

"I wish you would laugh like that all the time," she said, her eyes darting back and forth between mine. "I don't think I've ever heard anything so beautiful."

Fluttering filled my stomach. I almost kissed her, but everything in me said not to. Not yet. Not so early in the night when I was finally starting to enjoy being around someone again. I would save that for when I couldn't resist her any longer because the moment it happened, I would need to take her home and make her mine.

I started moving the wheel faster again, though in the opposite direction from what we'd been spinning in. Her laughter filled my ears again, and I sat there dumbfounded at the feelings running through me.

Chapter Six
Des

He laughed.

He fucking *laughed*.

I hadn't been able to keep my eyes off him. The sound of that laugh and how he looked at me made me want to kiss him right there. I nearly had, but I didn't want to spook him. And that slow moment we'd shared, how his soft beard had felt beneath my fingers… Fucking hell, I was in trouble.

I couldn't stop laughing as we stumbled out of the ride, his hand on my waist as he guided me toward the exit. Once we were out, I took a few steps away from him to try and catch my breath. The full moon caught my eye as I looked up, and just as my breaths began to even, I felt a warm body press flush to my back.

My knees weakened as I inhaled the musky scent of his cologne and resisted limping into his grasp. His hand tickled over my forearm, the touch so light that it sent a chill down my spine.

"What are you doing to me, princess?" he whispered in my hair.

"Breaking you," I said.

"It's working," he admitted. "I'm not sure I like it."

I turned around, finding him staring at me with such intensity in his gaze that I had to force myself to breathe. He reached up and pushed a hair wave

21

off my face before gently touching my jaw.

"I think you do like it," I said. "I think how much you like it is eating at your insides, breaking down that exterior one tap at a time."

"I won't go down without a fight," he said.

I bit my lip and grasped his arms, inching my face closer and closer to his. His throat bobbed as our noses grazed.

"Go ahead," I whispered. "Kiss me like I know you want to."

"Not here," he grunted. "Not yet."

Yet.

I took a step back at the word and pushed my hands into his, giving him a deliberate once over. "Okay, sunshine. We have five more tickets. What do you want to do next?"

Axel sighed and looked around us. "Tilt-a-Whirl."

Every ride Axel chose was more intense than the last. By the time we were down to two tickets, I had to pause and sink over my knees to keep from falling over from how dizzy I'd become.

Axel rubbed my back as I caught myself, and I swore I heard a soft laugh come from him.

"Alright?" he asked.

"I get to pick the next ride," I said after blowing out a few deep breaths.

"I didn't think you got nauseous on rides," he said.

"I don't," I replied as I straightened. "Dizzy, though, yes."

A smile lifted to his eyes, and my heart warmed at the sight. "I'll make it up to you later," he promised. "Where to next?"

"Ferris wheel," I said. "I want a long, slow ride to gather my wits."

"So that's how the princess likes it," he mocked. "Long and slow. Judging by how you screamed during the other rides, I thought maybe you like it hard and fast."

I stared at him, heat spreading from my stomach to between my thighs. "Hard and fast has its place. Can't a girl like both?" I managed.

Axel didn't reply. He looked to the ground, up the trail where the Ferris wheel was, and then he tugged my hand. "Ferris wheel. Then food."

The line for the ride was longer than the others, and it was primarily full of couples looking to go on the ride and make out, which, if I was being honest, was what I wanted too.

Yet.

That word kept ringing in my mind as I held close to him and laid my head on his shoulder, still steadying myself from the whirlwind of rides we'd just been on.

"Okay?" Axel asked.

"Yeah," I said. "Definitely need food soon."

His hand rubbed mine, and my stomach fluttered at the sincere gesture. "Starving," he muttered.

We reached the front of the line after a few minutes, and Axel sat with a heavy sigh when we stepped into the seats. I took a chance, sitting with one leg crossed to lean into him. The ride began to move, and he pushed his arm around the back of the seat behind me.

"This is my favorite view," I said when we reached the top.

"Mm…" His thumb rubbed my shoulder, though his eyes didn't leave the tree line.

"Do you know what I think?" I asked him as I moved further into his side, my hand now on the inside of his thigh.

His jaw ticked, but he didn't stop me. "What?"

"I think you're enjoying this." I rubbed my hand closer to the zipper of his jeans, seeing his stomach retract.

"Which part?" he asked as we passed the attendant and started going back up. "The carnival or what you're doing right now?"

I palmed the stiffness growing beneath my touch, feeling him twitch slightly. "Both," I said.

"Fuck," he cursed under his breath. "*Des...* Do you need me to admit I'm enjoying it?"

"It would be nice," I said. "But no. I can feel just how much you're enjoying this."

"Shit." He was stifling his need at that moment, but I didn't want him to. I wanted him released. Undone. "If you keep doing that—"

"What, Axel?" I dared. "What will you do?"

His eyes opened to mine, blazing fire in them, and I nudged his nose with my own. Every breath was a struggle to keep under control. Every centimeter between our lips now magnetized.

"Make me stop," I whispered.

He cursed again as his hand slid up my thigh and squeezed my waist. "Des..."

The ride stopped. We were near the ground, *too* near the ground for me to continue doing what I was doing without getting caught. I withdrew my hand from his lap and pulled back to look at his frustrated face. His tongue raked over his lips.

"The minx is afraid of getting caught?" he asked.

I scoffed at the tease. "Not hardly."

The ride began again, and when it was our turn to get off, I grabbed my raccoon prize and exited quickly.

"So," I said after walking a few feet. "What does my lumberjack want to do for our last ticket?" I looked around us to the other rides. "Tornado? The music ride that goes backward? Or does he want food—"

Axel gripped my hand and pulled me into him. That intensity was back in his gaze as he wrapped his hand around my waist and trapped me against his chest.

"You're going to pay for what you just did," he said in a low voice. "We're going on your teacups again."

I tried to keep my composure. "I thought it was a kid's ride," I remembered him saying.

Axel sighed as he glanced over my head and then back to me. "I'm curious."

"About?"

"About if anyone has ever made you come in public before."

I felt my eyes widen and thought maybe I hadn't heard him right. But judging by the desire in his eyes, I knew I wasn't mistaken.

"It's a favorite pastime," I said. "Usually only at the end of a bad date so I don't have to worry about having to make up some excuse to get him out of my bed."

Axel raised a brow. "So all the men I've seen come out of your door in the early morning?" he asked. "They were…"

"Decent dates," I said with a shrug. "Nothing special. Good enough for maybe one more round but dull enough that I usually forgot to call them back."

"And what kind of date would be with a man that made you come in public in the middle of the date?" he asked, his chin lifting as he held over me.

I raised my hands to his chest and curled my fingers into the soft, flannel shirt. "A fucking great one," I hissed.

I thought he might kiss me there, and dammit, I wanted him to. But he leaned down, too close to be without his lips on mine, and just when I closed my eyes in the hopes that he would finish closing that gap, he said, "You'll have two minutes to come, princess. No games like you were just playing with me. You'll come for me. Quietly. I don't want the attendants stopping my fun."

Heat surged between my thighs. I swallowed as I pulled back and smirked up at him. "You'll have two minutes to *make* me come, sunshine. I hope you're up for the challenge."

The smile nearly stayed on his lips that time. "Never challenge me. I always get what I want."

"You've met your competitive match then," I said. "Because I never lose." I braced myself on his biceps and pushed up on my toes. "Lucky for us, this is a game we can both win."

Chapter Seven
Axel

The low-hanging, orange fluorescent lights over the spinning ride snagged my vision as I pulled her by the hand toward it. All I could think about was how much I'd wanted to kiss her on the ride the first time—how much I wanted to kiss her right then, right there.

And that minx arousing me on the fucking Ferris wheel? A dark corner to drag her into and fuck her raw had looked appealing on the way back to these cups.

I didn't know how much longer I could wait. The tension between us had me on edge. I needed to touch her, to hear the soft noise I'd heard her make through the walls of her apartment so many times before. Though most of those idiots hadn't realized half of the time she was faking.

Poor fucking kids.

Des wrapped her arm into mine as we paused in the short line. I wasn't sure how exactly she'd pulled this out of me in a few hours. But it felt right. I looked down at her as she laid her chin on my arm. So fucking gorgeous there. The glow of the lights hit her face, making her mulberry hair and light pink lipstick stand out against her golden skin. Every inch of her glowed, and I couldn't wait to see her undone.

"You are a puzzle, Axel Connors," she said.

"Why?" I asked.

27

"I never would have guessed you were into public affections."

I turned my body into hers. "I'm not," I said. "When I finally kiss you, it'll be away from all these people."

"Why?"

"Because I won't be able to stop," I replied.

She swallowed as the words swept through her. "What if I kiss you now and don't give you a choice?"

"You don't want to do that," I said.

"Don't I?"

I shifted and leaned down into her ear. "All these people will watch as you come for me. Do you want to show them how you'll get on your knees and beg for my cock in your mouth too? Or would you rather sit on my lap in this ride while I fuck you from behind? Everyone will watch because I won't give you a chance to resist. Those are the options if you kiss me right now."

Des's brows lifted in surprise. "The second one," she said before wrapping her hands around my cheeks.

Before I could respond, and thankfully before she could kiss me, the ride attendant called us forward. I forced myself from her mesmerizing gaze and pulled her through the gate to one of the empty cups toward the middle. She was staring at me when I looked up, and I scooted in closer to her before tapping the seat at my side.

The ride slowly started up, and I placed a hand on her thigh and squeezed. "Whatever you do, keep spinning this wheel," I whispered in her ear.

Des turned my way as she placed her hands on the wheel. I slowly moved my hand higher and higher, careful to keep it discreet and not go wild at the sight of her blown pupils and heaving breaths.

"Relax for me," I said softly, shifting her skirt up. "It's just us."

Her face was so close that all it would have taken was a shift in the ride, and our lips would have met. But I didn't kiss her, and she didn't dare kiss me. I would lose all control of myself if I did, and I was savoring her like this.

I expected to find underwear or pantyhose covering her pussy, but—

"Fuck," I cursed into her shoulder. "They make crotchless pantyhose?"

She smirked like she had the best-kept secret. "Of course."

I groaned, resisting the urge to pinch her at the triumph on her face, and then I slipped a finger over her clit. Fucking hell, she was soaking. All that adrenaline, that teasing, she was drenched from it. I stifled the stiffening of my cock.

The smirk vanished from her lips, replaced with a bite. She slowed on the wheel at the distraction.

"Spin, baby," I whispered. "I want the world to be a blur as you come for me."

God, that little noise she made was intoxicating. I toyed with her clit, watching only the expression on her face, hearing only the soft sounds she was trying to keep under control. Her legs spread wider for me as she sank further into the seat.

My dick pressed against my zipper at how wet she was. As I slipped a finger inside her, I imagined it was my cock sliding in her, knowing how fucking good she would feel around me, and I cursed again.

Down, Axel, I told myself.

Though watching her didn't help my need. It fueled it. I pressed my thumb to her clit and swirled, pumping a finger slowly in and out of her. Her hips began to buck, arms bracing stiff against the wheel.

"Keep moving," I told her. "Faster. With me."

My pace picked up, and she began to spin us so quickly that the world truly did become a blur. Her soft moans were drowned out by the sound of laughter around us and the ride's engine. But I only saw her. I only saw her sucking on her lip, her bent knees and pointed ankles, and how she held her head back to the sky as pleasure seared through her.

"Fuck—Axel—"

"That's it," I said. "Come for me, Des. Let go."

She tightened around me, now squirming in the seat as we spun and spun. I was mesmerized by her, addicted to the way she moved, the way she sounded, the way she did as I asked.

Just as the ride's engine reached its peak, so did she. Adrenaline pulsed in my throbbing heart as she came around my finger. She released the wheel, one hand shooting to her hair, the other to my shoulder. Her hips rocked as she rode that wave, rode my hand down and down into her oblivion. And as she relaxed from her high, I withdrew my fingers, soaking with her release, and tasted her.

The ride was still going, slower now, but I had time to watch her collect herself. Watch her eyes open again, filled with satisfaction as she saw me licking my fingers. Her gaze weighed with lust at the sight.

"I—" The ride came to a slow halt before she could get the words out.

Her chest continued to heave, and she didn't move for a moment. She only stared at me, obviously forgetting about the rest of the people around us.

Until the ride attendant called for everyone to get off.

I reached for her hand and kissed her knuckles before standing and pulling her with me. Her first step was a wobble that I caught, almost making me smile at her weakened knees.

Her hair was a mess of waves from all the wind, from the orgasm still moving through her. After we walked a few feet away from the ride, I paused to pull her into me.

"What do you want to do now?" she asked as she braced her hands on my arms. "Throw axes? Win me another stuffed animal? Join in the pie eating contest? Fuck on the swings?"

Her mockery nearly made me smile. I paused in front of her, staring down at the most beautiful woman I'd ever seen. I had to swallow the dryness in my throat at the sight of the lighting around us, which seemed to bask only on her.

"I think I want to take you home," I said as I pushed her hair back. "I think if I have to stay here without kissing you much longer, I'll collapse."

Chapter Eight
Des

Shit, he'd said everything right. *Done* everything right.

Every fucking thing.

I was ready to give in completely. Go home? Fuck, yes. If it meant his touch again, if it meant finally kissing him...

"You poor thing. Tired of all the laughter?" I said, trying to keep my composure.

"Too many people," he grunted, and I almost laughed at the look he gave the bystanders around us.

I leaned up on my toes like I might kiss him but stopped short. "There are a few more things I have to have before we leave," I said.

"Really?" he asked as I pulled at his hand. "I thought the cups might have enticed you to leave sooner."

"Is that what that was about?" I asked. "Getting me hot and bothered so you could go back to your lonesome sanctuary early?"

"It's not lonesome if you're with me," he said.

I eyed him, but shook my head. "No, I can't leave this carnival without getting three things first: a funnel cake, apple cider whiskey cocktail with whipped foam, and a pumpkin spice latte with oat milk to go."

Axel squinted. "Pumpkin spice?"

"You don't get to make fun of me until you've tried it," I

said.

He yanked me by the hand back into his arms, enveloping me with his muscular body and his hands around my waist. My breath caught in my throat again, and I wondered if I'd ever get used to him pulling me toward him like that.

The thought stilled me, though. And it nearly prevented me from enjoying the rest of the night.

"You get your little latte and your cake, and I'll get the drinks," he said, his hands squeezing my waist. I was reminded of the way he squeezed my thigh on those spinning cups, and I was glad of the hold he had on me.

"And when we've finished our drinks, I'll take you home."

I shifted in his embrace. "What happens at home?"

"You get your cake here. I'll feast on mine when I lay you across your countertop."

My thighs tightened as I stifled my whimper. "How do you know I'm inviting you back to my place?" I forced myself to say.

He scoffed quietly. "Is this all you want tonight? Just the carnival?"

All I want.

I wanted a lot.

And judging by this date, I wasn't sure one night *was* all I wanted.

He'd been my neighbor for over a year. We'd passed glances in the hallways and interacted more times than I could count. I'd almost considered him a friend were it not for his unwillingness to open up. I'd always wondered what was beneath his hardened exterior, why he was the way he was. The way he'd always looked at me, like he hated the thoughts going through his head for daring to look.

And after tonight…

This had felt too right. This had been too comfortable. Every touch and word we'd spoken had felt completely normal. Even the silences had felt right. I knew if this night were to go further, if I went back to his place, spent the night, and tomorrow, if he looked at me as though it were nothing, I'd be broken.

Anyone else... Anyone else would have been easy. Anyone else would have made this simple.

But it was *him*.

"I'll meet you at the tables behind the Ferris wheel," I managed before letting him go.

The thoughts swirled in my head as I ordered my latte and cake. Distracting me so much that the beverage guy had to call out for me when the line moved.

Axel was waiting for me at the edge of the Ferris wheel line, two piping hot drinks in his hands. His tongue darted out to lick his bottom lip as his gaze lingered on my hips before moving back to my eyes.

"See something you like?" I asked him.

He didn't answer except with the brightness in his eyes. I jerked my chin toward the tables at the edge of the tree line.

"Come on. Best view for the fireworks," I said.

The walk to the tables was silent, and I took in the smell of the carnival, the trees, and the crisp autumn night air. A few delighted screams followed us from one of the more dramatic rides on the other side of the Ferris wheel, and I smiled as I sat on the top of the table.

"What?" he asked as he did the same.

"Do you remember being young and fearless?" I asked

him. "Full of adrenaline, like nothing could hurt you. Not even rides like the Tornado, which literally flips you upside down."

The softest chuckle sounded beside me, and I turned to see Axel almost smiling down at his cup. "Complete asshats," he said gruffly.

I choked out a laugh and broke off a piece of funnel cake. "Asshats?"

"My friends when we were younger." He took a swig of his drink, leaving foam behind on his mustache that melted away before I could do anything about it. "Shitheads, all of us. We'd take our bikes out on Halloween and ring random doorbells—"

"I think we all did that," I said, remembering my own rambunctious days. "I miss being that person."

He looked at me then. "Seem pretty fearless to me," he said.

"When I want to be," I agreed.

I pulled the sleeves of my sweater down over my hands as I hugged the warm apple cider whiskey cocktail to me. I inhaled the sweet scent, the cinnamon stick and the tang of whiskey. The hum of people laughing and talking seemed to drown away there. I turned to Axel and considered how his elbows were braced on his widespread knees, how his flannel shirt strained over his biceps, and how his grasp encompassed the seemingly small cup in his hand.

"Here—" I said, setting down my cup and grabbing the latte. "Try it." I held the pumpkin spice out to him, and he eyed me. I almost laughed. "Big burly man afraid he'll like pumpkin?" I mocked him.

The challenge irked him. He set down his whiskey and hesitantly took the latte from my hands. I watched him sniff it, watched the reluctance rise in his gaze, but he took a swig, and for a moment, I couldn't tell whether he liked it.

Jack Whitney

And then, he took another sip.

"You *like* it," I realized, my eyes widening.

"Mm… No—" He held the cup up and looked at it like he thought I'd lied about the flavor.

"Holy fuck, you like it," I repeated.

"I hate it," he said finally. "It's fucking awful."

"Liar."

He pinched my side as I took the drink from his hand, and I laughed, squirming away. But when I looked at him again, he was genuinely smiling. My heart melted to my stomach. It was so cute I almost said something about it, but I decided I wouldn't tell him and instead kept that image to myself.

Axel Connors, smiling and lying about liking a pumpkin spice latte.

I nudged him sideways and scooted closer just as the first firework blew into the sky. And for a few seconds, I forgot myself as I laid my head against his shoulder and hugged my whiskey drink back to my chest. All colors of fireworks blazed high above us, creating various designs and winding together to create a kaleidoscope of imagery.

Axel shifted in his seat, his arm wrapping around the back of me to my waist. My breath caught as he massaged my hip, and it took everything in me not to look up at his handsome face. I could feel his nose nuzzling in my hair, his hand traveling up beneath my sweater to draw circles on my bare skin.

I was a puddle on that table.

I wanted his hands everywhere.

I wanted his mouth everywhere.

I wanted him to bend me over the table and cover my mouth with his hand as he fucked me blind and the sound of the fireworks muffled my screams.

My legs squeezed at the fantasy just as his beard grazed my hair. But even as I started to reach to his thigh, the thoughts from earlier invaded my mind. His smile invaded my mind. And I was once more paralyzed that this one night would be it.

It wouldn't be enough for everything I wanted. Not enough of him, if there was even such a thing. I wanted more of this. More of his touch. More of his mouth. His rough hands. His body hard against mine. I wanted the feel of his beard scratching my sensitive thighs. His hands holding me in place and his words paralyzing me into the bed.

I wanted more dates like this. I wanted to get to know the real man behind that stern exterior. I wanted to know the man that few others knew. I wanted his days, his nights—all of them, or at least a chance.

"Axel..." My head rolled against his shoulder as he continued his soft movements. "Tell me what you want here."

"I want to take you home," he said in my hair. "I want to finish what we started back at those cups. I want to taste more of you. Take my time with you. Make you come over and over until you can't feel your own body."

I sank further into his arms, further under his spell.

"What do you want?" he asked.

"More than what you'll give me," I replied, my eyes still closed as I tried to memorize every second of this.

His finger tugged my chin to look at him, and I was met with his darkened, lustful gaze.

"How do you know what I'll give you?" he asked.

"Because I know you well enough to know that you haven't had a relationship in years," I said.

"Maybe things changed," he said before leaning forward. His lips brushed mine, and my heart dropped. I nearly gave in.

But I wanted more.

And I was terrified of getting hurt again.

"Why? Because you finger fucked me on some carnival ride?" I snapped.

He balked, letting go of my waist. "I thought you were looking for fun, like your usual dates," he argued. "Is it more than that?"

"With you? Yes," I admitted as I pushed off the table. "Anyone else, I would have been fine with a one-night stand. Anyone else, and I would have welcomed kicking him out of the apartment in the morning. But with you…"

Fireworks rocketed over the Ferris wheel, so loud they nearly drowned out my thoughts.

"Des…" Axel's hand grazed my own, but I jerked away from him.

"Don't," I forced myself to say. "Don't get my hopes up for something that means nothing to you."

He paused, and I watched him falter as he realized the words I'd just said.

I expected something… *anything*… to come from his lips—even a mocking retort. I would have welcomed the chance to fight or tease.

But I got nothing.

His silence made me scoff and hate myself for ever thinking that what I felt with him was different. I grabbed my purse from the table and hauled it over my shoulder as I stood.

"Des—"

"It's fine," I said quickly. "I should be…" I could barely get words out. I could barely catch my own feet. "I should be going anyway," I finally managed, locking eyes with him again. There was confusion written across his face, pain in his gaze.

"I'll see you around," I said. "Thanks for the drinks. This was… this was fun."

Axel stood, looking like he might reach for me, but I shook

my head and continued backward.

"Goodnight, Axel."

Chapter Nine
Axel

Idiot.

Stupid, fucking idiot.

I left the carnival in a rage, replaying her running across that fucking field over and over in my mind. I let her get away.

Why didn't you say anything?

I knew exactly why I hadn't said anything, and I drove around the city for an hour, trying to determine what to say to her when I did see her again. I couldn't let her go to bed thinking she meant so little. I had to tell her why. I had to let her know how she made me feel.

It was after midnight before I mustered up the courage to knock on her door. I'd come back and showered, paced the apartment repeatedly while my dog, Koko, stared at me like I'd lost my mind.

Which I felt like I had.

I was restless with what she might say, how she might react. She could have thrown a drink in my face or punched me, and I would have welcomed it.

The worst thing that could have happened was her not answering that door.

I knew she was home because her lights were on, and I could hear her water running from the sink and the sound of her television.

Everything I'd practiced saying on the drive vanished from my mind with that first knock.

"Des?" I called out when she didn't answer. "Des, please. Answer."

Silence.

My forehead sank to the door, and I knocked again. "Des, I'm not leaving until you answer."

A shadow moved on the other side—three more knocks. "Des, I need to talk to you. Come on. If you need me on my knees, I'll do it. Hit me. Throw things at me. Anything but this."

The door swung open, and I almost fell inside.

Pain filled her eyes when she looked at me and crossed her arms. She'd taken off her skirt and shirt and put on a short black robe over her pantyhose, her hair now pinned back in a large clip.

"What?" she asked.

My mind blanked seeing her there, knowing I had caused the pain in her expression.

"Speak, Axel," she snapped. "You wanted to talk. Talk."

"I don't... I forgot something tonight," I managed.

"What? You didn't give me anything to hold."

I saw that blue raccoon on the bar behind her, and a lump rose in my throat at the memory. "No. I forgot... I forgot this."

My lips crashed into hers, obviously catching her off-guard as I wrapped a hand around her cheek, the other around her waist. She staggered, but I held tight. My heart fell to my fluttering stomach, itching for her to open up, to put me out of my misery. I would have begged had she asked me to. I would have sank to my knees and asked her to forgive me for not doing this sooner.

She slowly softened into me, her hands moving up my

chest, and my body limped as her tongue slid against mine. I was nearly undone as a little moan left her, and she stretched on her toes, her arms wrapping behind my neck.

Why had I waited so long to do this?

The quick desperation faded into savoring as I backed us further into the room and slammed the door behind us. My hands roved over her back and up to her neck. I wanted every second to last an eternity. I could still taste the cinnamon on her tongue and smell the autumn breeze in her hair.

But she pushed my chest, and I stumbled as she looked up at me with regret in her eyes.

"Axel—"

"It could have been anyone tonight," I said before she could break my heart. "But it was you. It was *you*. The one person that drives me to near insanity. The one person that can turn my entire day upside down. Sometimes I can't breathe when I'm with you, and then when you're gone, I can't breathe without you. You are... You... *Fuck*." I cursed myself for the corner I'd found myself in, for not knowing how to say what she meant to me. Not knowing how to let her know—

"If I'd had the choice for that date tonight, I'd have picked anyone... *anyone* else... and yet, it was you," I said.

She flinched and took a solid step back. The vacancy of her body heat made my stomach drop. I could see the absolute devastation in her gaze, and it was all I could do to contain my frustration at my own choice of words.

"*What the fuck, Axel*," she hissed. "You think you can come in here and kiss me, then break my heart after I told you— " she swallowed, running her hands through her hair. "After I told you that I can't do 'nothing' with you, and now—"

"I would have picked anyone else because you scare the shit out of me," I admitted.

Saying it aloud, baring myself... agony swelled in my bones. I couldn't stop myself from faltering, running my hand through my hair as I slowly felt every wall around me slide.

"What are you talking about? Why do I scare you?" she asked.

I paused, looking her over and hating the pained way she was looking at me. "Because you're the only person that can get under my skin as you do," I told her fast. "Because with you, I know it's more than one kiss. I know it's more than one night. It's everything. It's a lifetime. And I am powerless against it."

Agony drained from her gaze, her chest rising with her jagged breaths. She shifted from foot to foot as she hugged her arms around herself, tongue darting over her lips. Those flushed lips. Fuck, I could barely think.

"Tell me how I drive you crazy," she said.

I swallowed against my dry mouth as I chanced a step forward. She didn't move away, so I moved closer. Close enough that I could reach her elbows to uncross her arms. Slowly. One word, one breath at a time.

"It's the way you blast your damn pop music and leave the door open while you dance around the kitchen," I started, the image placing itself in my mind. "It's every time you bring a man home, and I have to hear the sound of your moans for someone else. It's when you're so chipper in the mornings and talk to me in the elevator like we're friends. It's..." I settled, bracing myself around her as I continued.

"It's the way you sit on your balcony during the rain and look as though the world is falling apart around you," I said, and her eyes lifted to mine, a sadness in them that I never wanted to see again showing its bewildering face.

"It's how, in those moments, I don't know how to help you," I said softly.

She teetered on her feet as my hands ran slowly down her chilled arms. "I didn't know you saw me," she said.

"I always see you." My hands entwined with hers, hovering there, watching her gaze darken as she lifted her chin.

"Do you want me to stop doing those things?" she asked. "Would that make you hate me any less? Would that—"

"Never stop doing those things." My forehead met hers, and I closed my eyes to inhale the spiced vanilla and apple scent of the candle wafting around us. "I'm not very good with this," I said. "But I know I want you. I know I've wanted you since the day I moved in, but I was too afraid of what this could be, and I couldn't stand to get hurt again."

"You've hated me since that day," she said as she looked up at me.

I pushed her hair back off her face, noting the glint of amusement in her eyes. "Angry at the world," I said. "How else should I have reacted to a beautiful light showing up in my life and trying to drag me out of the darkness?"

A faint smile nearly reached her eyes, but it was gone in a flash, replaced by that same hurt that made my heart drop. I pressed myself flush against her, my palms bracing against the counter at her back. Her breath caught in her throat, and I dipped low, pressing my lips to her nose, to her cheek, to her jaw, eliciting the softest noise of ecstasy that I wanted to hear more of. She tasted like the cold night air, and I wanted her splayed on the counter so I could take my time tasting the rest of her.

"I'm not them, Des," I whispered in her ear, my teeth nipping at her earlobe. "I'm not some decent date that you have to throw out the next morning, some idiot that isn't going to take care of you. Give me a chance to show you you're more than one night. Give me a chance to show you everything."

She stiffened against me, her head turning slightly as she resisted. "You know, I think I'm really starting to hate you," she said as her gaze flickered up to mine. "You can't just say these things, Axel, and expect me to fall at your feet."

Chapter Ten
Des

Everything in me wanted to go to him, wanted to give in to him. But... I couldn't.

He shifted on his feet, tongue darting out over his lips as he reached for my neck. The simple touch of his thumb dragging over my cheek made my eyes roll.

"Tell me how much you hate me," came his subtle rasp.

"So much," I managed.

"How much, princess," he said. Lower and lower, his fingers trailed, pausing just below my breast, that thumb brushing over my clothed nipple. "Does it enrage you to know how much you're aching for me right now?"

It really did.

"You don't know what you're talking about," I argued, though as he softly cupped my breast, my knees began to weaken.

"No?" He leaned down, and I forgot to breathe as his beard tickled my skin, his lips grazing my throat. Shit, that beard. I wanted to feel it on the soft of my thighs and igniting every inch of sensitive skin on my body.

"Give me a chance," he whispered, sending chills over my arms. "Let me prove how much I want this. How much I want you."

My forehead rolled against his. My every muscle was

restless with desire. Suddenly, I was back on those spinning cups, forcing myself to keep spinning the wheel as his fingers slid between my thighs. The rushing memory flooded me down to my heated center, and I let out a whimper.

His hands trailed down my sides to my hips, where he squeezed just enough to elicit an audible moan from my throat.

"That sound…" His desperate voice raked over me as his lips landed on my jaw. "How else can I make you do that?" He cupped my ass firmly, scrunching my robe between his fingers and straightening over me. Green eyes burning through me, I couldn't help the hand I pushed up to his chest.

I was aching for him, wet from just his touch on my clothed skin.

He moved his hand from my ass over my thigh. His lips were so close to mine that I could feel his breath on my cheek. Every inch of his fingers closer to my pussy had me once more forgetting how to breathe. And when he slipped a finger between my clothed thighs, I lifted my leg around his hips.

"Fuck, Des," he muttered, cursing against my lips. "Are you sure you hate me?"

My hips bucked into his hand, and I curled a hand around his neck. "Yes," I managed.

The corner of his lips flinched upward. "Tell me why," he said as he slowly delved between the slit of my stockings and began his tease. Dragging that finger up and down my drenched pussy. Fuck me, I was falling again. I couldn't help it. The way my body reacted to him was instinct. Like he could draw out every urge I'd ever had.

"I hate the way you look at me," I said, my voice struggling. "I hate…" He pressed harder, making my hips shift. "I hate—fuck, Axel—" His expression hadn't changed.

God, I needed him to fuck me before I exploded with anticipation.

"I hate the way you're teasing me right now." My grip on his shoulders tightened. "I hate how much I want you."

"Tell me what you want from me," he said, and I felt as he nudged my thighs open wider, clenched my ass, and slid a finger over my clit.

"Shit, princess," he muttered, and I knew I was done for. I knew he was feeling just how much I truly wanted him, how much I needed him to skip this tease and fuck me backward over this counter.

My fists tightened into his shirt as I held on, my hips bucking at their own pace, my moan echoing around the kitchen.

"That's it," he said before kissing my throat. "Take it. Tell me what you want me to do to you. Ride my hand."

"I want you buried inside me," I said, unable to keep it contained. "I want you to taste what you do to me every day when you look at me like you do. I want—*fuck*—I want *you*." His finger slipped inside me at the word, thumb pressing against my clit, and he lifted his head to look at me.

I couldn't breathe as he delved deeper and added a finger. Pleasure rocked through me. "Axel…" I practically cried out his name, *begged* his name.

His fingers stilled within me. Deep. Deeper than he'd reached on those cups. "Are you saying I can have you?" he asked.

"Yes," I practically begged. "Yes. Fucking take everything."

"Oh, thank fuck."

His lips crashed into mine. Desperate. Flooding. Consuming. Tongues sweeping, I held onto him as he pulled from within me and then placed my ass on the countertop. I couldn't stop kissing him as I reached for his shirt, discarding it to the ground. I groaned into his mouth at the ecstasy of our bodies flush, his full muscles against me. And once he'd pulled my pantyhose down and taken them off my legs, he shoved my back onto the countertop. I started to reach for the belt of my robe, but he grabbed my hand.

"No, baby," he said with a tut of his tongue. "Let me unravel you tonight. I've fantasized about having you for too long to let you undo yourself. You'll come for me until I've taken every last moan from your body."

Chills erupted on my skin, sending my breaths into stitches as he leaned over and placed a kiss between my breasts. He slowly undid the tie of my belt, then pushed my robe open. A low groan came from within him at the sight of my naked body lying there, waiting for him and only him. "You're so fucking gorgeous," he said before kissing my hips. "I'm going to have you every way I can tonight," he swore. "And then after I've bathed you and fed you... I'll fuck you over the railing outside as we watch the sun come up."

"I didn't know you were also a romantic," I said with a smirk.

Axel yanked me by the thighs, pulling my ass to the very edge of the counter, and I watched as a crooked smile spread over his lips. He dug those fingers into my skin, hard enough that I sucked in a sharp breath, my bottom lip sagging slightly. He reached up to my breast, palming it harshly, *deliciously*, making my chest arch and my hips roll against his.

His soft chuckle raked over me as he took in my body one inch at a time. "You know, I love you like this, Des." He leaned over, his breath tickling my hardened nipple. I started to wrap my hand around his neck upon his tongue flicking over me, but he grabbed my wrist again.

"Lift your arms and grab the edge of the counter behind you," he told me. I did, apprehensive about his not letting me touch him, but I didn't question it. He laid a kiss on my lips as I gripped the edge and then hovered over me for a moment.

"Don't let go."

He grabbed the backs of my thighs again, splaying me on the table, and sank low.

I tried to keep my composure as I watched him bend between my thighs.

"Fuck, you're everything I imagined you would be," he muttered, and I wasn't entirely sure I could even speak as his breath pulsed against my wetness. His tongue darted out once, licking over my clit, and I let out an uncontainable whimper.

He groaned against my center, the tip of that devious tongue raking up my middle. "Fuck, baby. Your taste—" My fingers gripped the edge of the counter, hips rocking as he teased. Shit, that fucking tongue. He reached behind him and pulled himself up a chair, putting him at direct access to feast as he pleased.

My feet latched atop his shoulders, and he held my hips in place as he continued to suck on my clit and run that tongue up and down, sometimes dipping inside me. His groans of satisfaction matched mine—as if he were eating his favorite dessert, and it had been made just the way he liked it.

I wanted to grab his hair and hold on. My arms struggled to stay up, so much that I had to grip the lip even harder to keep myself from falling apart. Fuck, he felt good.

I wasn't prepared for the orgasm cresting over me, wasn't ready to part from the deliciousness of his tongue fuck.

"Axel—shit, slow down," I begged. "I'm not ready to—*fuck me*—" my head rolled to the side, and I bit the inside of my arm to keep from screaming. "You feel so fucking good. Slow down—"

He did, and I sank into the counter at the savoring way he tasted me then. I let out an elongated curse, feeling him chuckle against my clit.

"Long and slow," he whispered before blowing against my wetness. "That's how you like it, baby?"

"Shit, yes," I groaned, eyes closed as I arched to the ceiling. His left hand moved from my thigh, the other moving up my stomach. And as he slipped a finger inside me, he cupped my breast firmly. My toes curled around the back of his shoulders, straining so much that I thought I might get a cramp in my calf.

Every suck and thrust limped me further until that orgasm began to wind up again, and I began to squirm. I knew he could feel me tightening by his smirk of satisfaction. I glanced down at him, and it was nearly my undoing. Those eyes held me. I couldn't look away, and he knew it.

Ever so slightly, his pace picked up. My head fell hard against the counter as I strained and strained. I was tipping over the edge of that wave, barely able to breathe.

"That's it," he said. "Come for me, princess."

I cursed to the ceiling, my hips bucking erratically as he tried to hold me down. But I couldn't stop it. I came. Stars filled my vision. I cried out louder than I ever had for any man, and he didn't stop licking me until I began to jerk out of his grasp.

He laughed deeply, sending a shiver down my spine as he stood over me a few seconds later. "You taste just as good as I thought you would," he said. He grabbed my wrists and pulled me upright, his thumb going to wipe the mascara from beneath my left eye.

Despite my tired arms, I didn't want him to stop. I wanted him to touch me everywhere. No breaks. No waiting. I needed him then. I'd waited too long to have him, and if he felt the same as me...

"I want you," I said. "I want you in the bedroom. I want to taste you and ride you, and then you hold me backward until

I have no feeling left in my legs, and I beg you for relief," I said. "And anything else you want to do to me. I'm yours."

Axel's brows raised, and he grabbed me by the thighs, hoisting me onto his waist as if I weighed nothing. His body swallowed mine, and I relished the feeling of being small in someone's arms.

"Yeah, you fucking are," he said before slapping my ass hard enough that the sting of it rippled over my entire body.

Chapter Eleven

Axel

I could still taste her on my tongue. Her lips met mine in a needing kiss as I moved us through the apartment to her bedroom. I couldn't believe I was holding her, kissing her, taking her, and making her mine.

There were so many fantasies I wanted to fulfill with her, and I wondered how far her desire went. How far she would let me go.

She moaned in my mouth as I smacked her ass again and grabbed the wealth of it. Her bare breasts pushed into my chest. A low groan escaped me at the feeling of her taut nipples against my skin. Fuck, I couldn't wait to suck and tease and fuck her delicious tits.

She raked her nails over my cheeks, down to my neck. Her robe fell to the ground, and I unclasped her hair from the updo, causing those soft locks to fall sideways over her shoulder, over my shoulder.

"I want you in my mouth," she muttered against my lips. "Let me taste you like you tasted me."

Shit, I wanted that too.

I threw her onto the bed and straightened at the end, unbuttoning my jeans. Her bottom lip drew behind her teeth as she watched me. She spread her legs and showed me her glistening pussy again, but just when I thought she would sit up on her knees, she laid down with her head at the end of the bed, ass exposed to the ceiling.

I slipped my jeans and boxers off, my stiff cock bobbing free. Her eyes widened, a mix of surprise and hunger filling her gaze.

"Axel Connors..." she cooed with a smile as her lashes lifted and our eyes met, but she didn't comment more. Instead, she turned over to her back, her head craned and falling over the bed.

I paused at the end of the bed and began to stroke my erect cock slowly. The desire in her gaze, the way her breasts were peaked, the stretch of her neck as she stuck her tongue out waiting for me... fuck, I didn't know how long I would last with her like this.

"Is this what you want?" I asked, tapping my cock on her awaiting tongue.

She groaned, closing her lips quickly, but only quick enough to graze my tip. *Shit*. Her chest rose off the bed as she arched to reach me, her hands going for the backs of my thighs. I reached for her neck, slowly dragging a finger down the column of it.

"Open wide, baby," I said. "Relax that throat. You're going to take all of me."

A small whimper escaped her, but she stuck her tongue out once more. I massaged her throat again and stared down at her, then watched as she began to take me in her mouth.

God, that was beautiful. The tip of my stiff dick disappeared behind her pink-tinted lips. She sucked, tongue running over the slit and making me wish I had a wall to grab. Bit by bit, I slowly let her adjust, saw her throat resisting, and felt her choke.

I stroked her jaw, palmed her breast. "That's it," was all I could manage.

Her cheeks hollowed out with every suck. Dammit, her

wet mouth and tongue had me straining--this *view* had me straining. She squeezed her thighs together like taking my cock made her pussy throb. I pinched her peaked nipple between my fingers, making her moan vibrate around my dick, and I cursed the room. Her fingers tightened on the backs of my thighs, pushing in more of me, and I obliged, pulling out slightly and then thrusting further down her pretty throat. She nearly had all of me in. Saliva dribbled from the sides of her lips as she choked.

I was going to lose my mind if I didn't fuck her mouth soon. This slow torture had me restless. And when she reached between my legs and toyed with my balls, a shudder ran through me.

"I'm going to lose it if you keep doing that," I muttered.

She groaned around my dick, pinching my sack, and I drove deeper inside her. Her nails scratched my leg, but dammit, she felt too good. Every suck and lick of her tongue, every time I felt her gag, only made me wilder for her, to the point that I lost myself in the moment and began to pick up my pace.

"Fuck, that's right, Des... choke, baby."

Her moan strummed over me, making me curse again. "Keep doing that," I said. "Hum a little song for me."

I felt her struggling for breath and saw her body beginning to squirm, but she did what I asked. I didn't know what song it was, but it was the most beautiful feeling and sound I'd ever heard. The vibrations only stopped when I sank so far down her throat that she couldn't breathe, and after a few more seconds, after nearly succumbing to that edge, I pulled completely out of her.

She gasped for breath as I picked her head up and cradled her heaving body into a sitting position. Sitting on the bed at her side, I reached up to her face, wiped the drool off her mouth, and saw that lipstick smeared so beautifully around her full lips. She looked at me in a daze, obviously coming back from the air deprivation.

"Shhh, baby," I whispered, kissing her neck. "I've got you."

A quiet moan left her, her forehead sinking against mine, and as she kissed me, she reached to stroke my still-wet cock. Her kiss was needing, consuming, and made me want to say to hell with this long and slow tease she had me doing.

I wanted to fuck the pussy I'd tasted until she screamed.

I pulled her straddle onto my lap. Her wetness grazed my throbbing dick, and the little moan that escaped her had me on the verge of spanking her ass red.

"Are you on—"

"Axel, if you don't fuck me right now," she said in a desperate voice. "Yes, I'm on the pill. Now give me that big cock of yours—Ah!—"

I picked her up and flipped her onto her back further up the bed. She leaned up, grabbed me by the neck to kiss me again, and then rolled me to my back. One leg sinking on either side of me, she pressed her palms into my chest and positioned herself atop me.

And then she slid—one shift at a time onto my dick.

"Oh my god," she hissed, her eyes shut as she readjusted and slowly worked herself onto me. I grabbed her hips, lifting my own, and she cried out at the fill. Fuck, she was tight around me. So fucking wet. God, she was soaking. This was better than I'd fantasized. This was ecstasy and heaven.

Buried halfway inside her, I strained at how much I wanted to hold her ass and drive deeper. As her hips began to move, I met her stroke for stroke. Watching her grab her hair and arch her back as she found her pleasure had me on edge again. She was a goddess on my lap. I didn't know how long I was going to last being able to watch her tits as they bounced, see her face scrunched up from my filling her, from the pleasure she was finding on my cock.

I moved my hands to her breasts, and her own hands settled atop mine as her mouth opened wide, letting out a slew of curses, moans, and high-pitched noises that I devoted to memory.

"Axel." My name was a strain, and with one more move, she took me completely in.

"Shit, baby," I muttered. Faster and faster, she rode me, almost limping when I moved my hands back to her hips. She had found that edge, found exactly where she wanted me, and she was falling.

"Oh God," she cried. "I'm coming—ah, fuck, Axel, I'm coming—"

I'd never heard her voice so high-pitched, so desperate and pleading. Her hands braced on my chest again, nails digging into my skin as she drove and rocked faster on my dick. God, I was done for. I felt her walls closing, her body beginning to shake.

She came with a strained noise I'd never heard anyone make, collapsing against my chest as she rode her wave of pleasure. I reached up and cupped her face in my hand, seeing the delighted devastation in her tear-filled gaze, and then I bent my knees up.

"Don't move, baby," I told her. "Let me ride this with you."

I thrust my hips upward and slammed into her again and again. Her face scrunched, her moans unable to cease, and I felt her coming apart again.

"Axel— fuck, I can't—"

"Shit, Des." My end was near. I was on the verge of exploding inside her. I couldn't stop it—

My entire body stilled and shuddered as I let go, releasing all that I had inside her tight cunt. Her lips crashed into mine as my dick throbbed and cum filled her.

She didn't move from atop me, even when my last groan had slowly dwindled, drowned behind her kiss. She stayed there, our kiss slowing as I pushed her messy hair off her face and finally met her satiated gaze.

"How are you even more beautiful right now?" I asked without thinking.

She twisted her head, kissed my palm, and then shifted to lay down on my chest. My breaths were a struggle, but I held her there and stroked her hair.

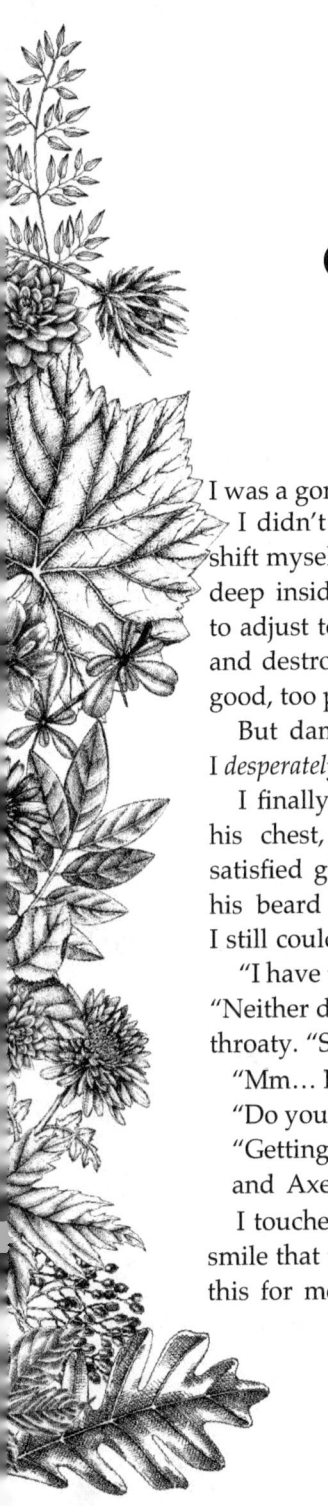

Chapter Twelve
Des

I was a goner.

I didn't want to move from atop him, let alone shift myself off his thick cock still buried so damn deep inside me. God, that had taken a few strokes to adjust to. My throat was raw, my pussy swollen and destroyed. I didn't want to get up. He felt too good, too perfect.

But dammit, I needed water. And I *desperately* needed to use the bathroom.

I finally leaned on my elbows, bracing them on his chest, and he looked up at me with that satisfied glow. I couldn't help toying slowly with his beard as his hands began to stroke my back. I still couldn't get over how small I felt atop him.

"I have to get up," I said. "But I don't want to."

"Neither do I," he replied, his voice rough and throaty. "So don't," he added.

"Mm… I have to," I complained.

"Do you need help?"

"Getting off this cock of yours? Yes, I might," and Axel smirked at the comment.

I touched his lips as they lifted that smirk into a smile that truly met his eyes. "I'm glad you'll do this for me," I said about the smile.

His lips met my cheek as he gave my tender ass a firm slap. "Only for you, princess."

I sat up and lifted, pulling slowly off his cock and feeling empty upon standing. Robe in hand, I went to the bathroom and locked the door behind me. I could already feel his cum starting to drag down my thigh, and I quickly used the toilet.

God, I was a mess.

One look in that mirror had me cringing. And he thought I was beautiful like this? Though, the more I looked at how disheveled I was—the messy hair, the mascara beneath my eyes, the red marks on my collar, and the blush on my ass... Maybe he thought it was sexy because he'd made me look like this. Because he had marked me. He'd made me a disarrayed jumble of waning makeup and frizzed hair.

I tried to compose myself the best I could before going back out into the bedroom, where I found Axel lying on the bed naked, thick dick on display between his muscular legs, his dark chest hair lightly covering that thick chest, hand behind his head—

And my rose sex toy in his hand.

My brows elevated at him twirling the thing in his hand. "I didn't know you were a snooper, Axel."

"Your drawer was open," he said before reaching to the nightstand and picking up a glass of water. "Drink."

I hadn't realized how long I'd been in the bathroom. Long enough for him to retrieve water from the kitchen, get comfy once more on the bed, and look in my nightstand drawer.

I hugged my robe around my chest and took the water from his hand. Fuck, it was cold, and it felt amazing on my raw throat.

"Did I hurt you?" he asked, and I discerned why he was asking—I was rubbing my neck in an almost comforting way like I could heal it from the outside.

I gave him a small smile. "I'm okay," I told him. "I'll have some hot tea for breakfast."

I walked around and sat the water on the bedside table before crawling into bed and sitting at his side. I hugged my knees to my chest, unable to look away from him as he began trying out the different settings on the rose against his palm.

"This is usually when you kick your dates out," he said as if he knew my routine.

"Stalker, much?" I teased him.

He didn't meet my eyes, but his lips twitched. "Hard not to pay attention when your fake screams sound like a bad porno."

My mouth dropped, and I shoved him sideways. A smile split his lips, mischief in his gaze. I shook my head at how pleased he was. "Ass," I said before taking another sip of water.

"This is for after all the decent dates have left?" he asked as he held up the toy.

"All the dates, really," I admitted. "Very few know what they're doing. It's good to have a back-up just in case."

He pressed it back to his palm, going through the settings again. "What's your favorite?"

I laid down on the pillow at his side and propped my head on my elbow. "Ah... I think it's the fifth one. Usually takes a little longer to finish me off, but I like how it feels."

He pressed the button five times and tested it on his hand. I wondered what he was thinking, if he was taking tips from the toy or if he, like some men, was turned off by it.

"Does it intimidate you?" I asked. "Make you feel smaller or inadequate?"

"Should it?" he asked.

"Some men think the toys are why it's hard to get us off."

"Idiots," he grunted. "Those aren't men, they're boys. Only someone so selfish would see this as competition and not a tool." He turned his head and met my eyes. "Let me show

61

you."

The notion took me aback. "You want to use it?"

Axel shifted onto his side and started removing my robe. "Have you ever thought of me while using it?" he asked as the silk fell off my shoulder. The backs of his fingers raked over my cheek, down my neck, all the way to my breast, where he paused to cup one.

"Yes," I managed as I laid on my back, bringing my arm behind my head and opening up to him. His lips landed on my taut nipple, sucking and nipping it while massaging the other. I loved the way he did that, so much that my back arched into his touch, and I had to tighten my thighs together again when I felt his cock stiffening at my side.

He leaned up level with me then, hand still massaging my tit. "I'm going to fuck you from behind, Des," he said, the tone of his voice dropping. "And I'm going to use this rose on your clit while I take my time filling you."

I almost cursed, my eyes closing at the fantasy. I barely lasted more than a couple of minutes with just that rose on me. To feel it going while his cock filled me... *Fucking hell.*

I remembered his promise to take every last moan from my body, and I was sure he was about to do that.

"How does that sound?" he asked before licking at my neck.

My hands curled around his head, raking through his dark hair. "Sounds like a dream," I muttered.

A smirk flashed in his eyes as he jerked his chin toward me. "Turn around."

I twisted in his arms until my back was against his broad chest. He nuzzled into the crook of my neck and began biting at my skin, his dick stiffening behind me. His lips landed on my shoulder, my neck, and I rocked my ass against his cock. He slipped his arm beneath my rib and reached over to palm my breast.

"I love these," he said on my throat, his other hand delving between my thighs. "Fuck, Des. You're so ready for me."

I pressed my ass against his hips, letting him hold me securely as he reached around and pulled my thigh. My legs opened, the one wrapping around the back of his, and the tip of his dick slid inside me. My bottom lip sucked behind my teeth as I moaned and tried to relax for him to enter.

"Your body was meant to be filled like this," he said, massaging my breast. "You were meant to be savored and tasted and claimed by someone that gives a damn about your pleasure," he continued, now sliding slowly in and out, each deliberate thrust deeper than the last. "I'll make you come like this every day, in every way you've ever imagined."

"Promise?" I managed.

He kissed my neck. "I swear, baby," he whispered. "Your pussy will only remember my cock from now on. You're mine to please."

"Yes," I groaned out, my eyes closing.

I felt him shift but was so consumed by the delicious rhythm of his dick that I didn't notice the toy coming into play until I heard the vibrating noise. I limped with anticipation and then jumped when he touched it to my stomach.

It was as if my body knew it was about to be destroyed. My pussy throbbed around his dick, and I tried not to open my eyes as he moved the toy lower and lower. I shrank against him, not sure what to do with my hands.

His middle finger touched my clit, making me flinch, and then he moved the toy directly over the very place even I had trouble getting right sometimes. But fuck, he got it right. He got it *so* right.

"Axel," I moaned out as he changed the setting.

"—three, four…" He let that staccato suction settle on me for a brief second before clicking the button once more.

"Five," he whispered in my ear.

God, I was doomed.

His hand wrapped up around my throat as he sucked my collar. My entire body was his to do with as he pleased. I was trapped against that strong hold, his elbow keeping my open leg in place as he let the rose work on my clit. I jerked with every vibration, the sensation of his dick filling me and that suction driving me insane. I couldn't see straight, could barely breathe. My hand tightened on his forearm, nails digging into his skin.

"If it's too much, say 'carnival'," he whispered.

I reached up and grabbed the back of his head, my body rolling against him. "Never," I hissed back.

He chuckled against my throat. "So stubborn," he teased.

I barely heard him. I fought through the feeling of falling, of not being in control, and found myself still fighting on the other side. I couldn't keep it at bay. I couldn't open my eyes. His thumb and forefinger pressed in on my throat, making me gasp, making my body tighten and tighten. I thought I might explode.

My orgasm crashed over me. I shuddered and jerked against his hold, spilling over his cock and making noises I'd never heard myself make. He moved the rose from my clit and held me tighter, stroking my side in a comforting way. A low groan and curse left him, but he didn't move from within me.

"So fucking beautiful," he muttered, his nose dragging over my cheek. "How will you do with a different setting?" he asked, more to himself. "Will you give me another orgasm?"

"I don't… *Axel*—"

I thought he would immediately place that rose back on my clit, but he didn't. Not at once. He moved that hand from my hip to my ass, giving it a loud smack that ricocheted through me before he grabbed me beneath the thigh and held my leg in the air.

His pelvis hit my ass with his next thrust, his dick all the way inside me, and then I felt him grab the toy again. I didn't count what setting he found that he liked, but when he put it to my clit, I couldn't stop the tear that ran down my cheek. The vibrations were fast. Fast enough that, combined with the new steady pace of his thrusts, I knew I was about to become a puddle.

My orgasm built and built. Every plunge of his cock made me cry out. I stopped feeling my body. All that was left of me was the mess of a girl who once thought herself invincible. I wished I'd had a mirror to see how messy I was. My thigh hiked high, his dick thrusting in and out, the sound of how wet I was echoing around the room, the toy on my clit, the tears streaking down my scrunched face.

Words left me. Though, I wasn't sure *what* words. Whether it was his name, God's, a slew of curse words, or incoherent babble, I didn't know. Every muscle in me strained trying to find some composure, but I was done.

Chapter Thirteen
Axel

She was even more beautiful when she slept.

That last orgasm had put her down. She'd fallen asleep almost immediately after I'd pulled out of her. I'd wrapped her in her blanket and decided to make her a snack while she slept.

Des had four things in her fridge: wine, salsa, cheese, and chicken.

I smiled at that. The tortillas in her cabinet caught my eye, so I cranked up her oven and made cheese quesadillas. I had a few things in my apartment that would have made them better. Once they were cooked, I turned the oven off and left them in the warming tray before stepping across the hall. Des was still asleep; for how long, I wasn't sure, but I figured I had enough time to grab a few things.

My apartment was minimalistic, not full of the fall decorations as she had. I barely had furniture other than the basics, but food…

I had food.

I decided I'd take Koko, my German Shepherd, out for a quick walk and take a quick shower while I was there. I could still smell the carnival on me. Dirt, sweat, and sex. I hoped she was still asleep when I returned and didn't think I'd left her entirely.

Koko was asleep on the couch when I entered.

"Hey, lady," I said as she slowly rose off the couch and stretched her limbs. I smiled at the old girl and gave her fluffy cheeks a scratch before getting her leash on, and then we took a couple of turns outside around the block.

When we returned, Koko took her treat—as usual—and curled back in her favorite spot, leaving me to chuckle at her and then take a quick shower.

Changing into sweatpants and a white tee, I grabbed my baseball hat and sat it backward on my head before grabbing sour cream, hot sauce, beer, and lettuce and then heading over to Des's place again.

The door was locked.

I frowned and knocked. "Des?" I called for her.

A shadow moved beneath the door before it swung open. She looked surprised to see me there.

"I thought you'd left," she said, her voice smaller than I was used to.

"You were asleep," I said. "Koko needed to piss. And—" I held up the ingredients in my hands "—I thought I'd make us food and take a shower."

She eyed the things in my hands before stepping aside to let me in. I laid the extra stuff I'd brought over on the counter, still watching her closely. "What is it?" I asked.

"Nothing," she said before stepping up to me and kissing my cheek. "I think I'll shower too."

She stalked away before I could say anything else, leaving me confused, but I didn't press it.

As she showered, I took the quesadillas out of the oven and began prepping our makeshift feast. I'd nearly finished when I heard her come out of the bedroom again, and I had to stop cutting the lettuce as I saw her.

She was wearing pink silk shorts and a snug white tee that showed off her midsection. Her mulberry hair had been brushed, her makeup tidied up, but still smudged a little at the creases of her eyes. She could have walked out of there with sopping wet hair and makeup running down her face, and I'd have still thought her the most beautiful thing to walk this earth.

But dammit, I really liked those shorts.

"Did you ever eat tonight?" she asked.

"I didn't," I replied.

She stepped beside me, her arm brushing mine as she observed the food. "I didn't know you were a chef," she said.

"I know my way around a kitchen," I replied. "And you barely had food in the fridge."

"That's because I keep the cabinets stocked with other fun things that are easy to grab on the go—" She went to her pantry and opened it up, revealing a slew of easy prep meals, snacks, and oatmeal.

I frowned at her definition of food. "We have to get you fresh food," I said.

Her lips twisted like she was fighting a smile. "Are you going to make it for me?"

She was too fucking cute like that. "Maybe if you're a good girl, I'll include you a few meals in my prep tomorrow."

The smile slipped from her face. "Fuck off. You're a meal prepper?"

"Only when I have to travel for the week."

"I didn't realize you traveled."

"Construction work. Travel to where the jobs are," I said with a shrug. I brushed my hands off and presented the tray of food to her. She hopped up on the counter and crossed her legs, and I sat on one of her barstools.

"I don't think anyone has ever cooked for me before," she said as she grabbed a cut of the quesadilla and dipped it in sour cream and salsa. "Boyfriend-wise, I mean."

"Boys being the correct term," I mumbled, shaking my

head at how these idiots had treated her.

She smiled as she chewed. "So then, what about you? Your exes," she asked me. "Were they as terrible as mine?"

My chewing slowed, and I took a sip of the beer I'd brought over. "We don't have to talk about them," I said. "We can just be us."

"That bad?"

I thought about the last woman I'd fallen in love with and how it had ended—how I'd *been* after it ended.

And how much I wanted to talk to Des about it.

"I moved across the country after her," I admitted.

Des slowly put down her cup of water. "That's why you came here?"

"I came here to start new," I said, staring down at my drink. "I thought if I got away from everything that reminded me of her, I'd be able to breathe again."

"Did it work?"

"Not at first. After a while, though... I never thought I would find anyone else that made me feel like that again."

"Like what?"

"Like life actually meant something," I said. "Like waking up was a good thing and not just a mechanical response of being alive. After we broke up, I couldn't function. The only thing that got me out of bed was my work. So, I sold my company and moved here." I took another swig of my drink and finally met her eyes. "And then I met you."

She swallowed at the statement, her head tilting. I shook my head and held up a finger before she could ask anything.

"I stayed away from you because I felt so drawn to you," I told her. "Because you were able to get under my skin so easily, and it scared me how much I wanted to let you in."

"Just me?" she asked.

"Just you."

"You've been a crab to me and the entire world because

you were scared to talk to me?" she asked, and I could hear the amusement in her tone.

"The rest of the world can kiss my ass," I grunted. "They deserve it. You don't."

Des took a long drink of water, considering me, and she hopped off the counter. She sank straddle over my lap. I sat my beer down before running my hands over the soft silk covering her ass, grabbing the fabric in my hands as she wrapped her arms around my neck.

"I think I like having you smiling all to myself," she said, her finger running over my beard. "And as far as your ex goes... she's an idiot for letting get away. But I'm glad she did. Because now—" her hips rocked into my lap, and I squeezed her "—now, you're mine."

I held her tighter as my heart began to thud in my ears, and then her lips landed on mine.

Soft and healing all at once. The way her tongue slid against mine, how her nails scratched my neck, and she moved against my lap...

This was the kiss I would say to hell with the world for.

I stood, picked her up by the ass, and moved us into the bedroom again.

She dropped down to her feet and pulled her shirt over her head before I could tell her to wait, then pulled at mine. But I grabbed her wrists before she could take those cute shorts off.

"Let me," I said.

Her dark eyes widened with her smile. I kissed her again, more desperate this time, and bent to consume the rest of her. Her neck, her collar, her chest... Falling to my knees to suck on her full breasts once again. She'd bathed in some fall scent I was sure she'd only bought for this season. I fully expected her to taste like snow at Christmas, chocolate on Valentine's, like peonies in the spring.

And I couldn't wait to delve into her.

I slipped my thumbs into those perfect silk shorts and slowly tugged them down. "I love these," I told her before kissing her navel. "These shorts will end me."

Her soft laugh filled my ears as the rest of her was exposed to me. She sat at the edge of the bed, letting me take her leg in my hand and kiss up her foot, her calf, the inside of her thigh. Her head fell back with a moan when I kissed her clit. I had to pull myself back from tongue fucking her there. I had another plan for her.

"Scoot up and grab the headboard, baby," I said as I stood.

She looked back at me, confusion in her eyes. "What?"

I resisted a laugh and crawled onto the bed, lying on my back on her pillows. "I want your pussy on my tongue, your ass on my face," I said when she sat up beside me. "It's almost sunrise. I have more to pull from this body."

She whimpered, her bottom lip sagging. "I don't know how much more you're getting from me, Axel. My thighs—"

"Are mine," I said, taking her chin in my fingers. "Every shake, every bruise I put on them, every orgasm that comes from between them. *Mine*. And when you can't feel them tomorrow, you'll have your choice of my name, my tongue, or my cock to blame for it."

Des swallowed. "Then leave on the hat," she said.

My gaze narrowed, and Des straddled over me. I grasped her ass firmly in my hands. "Leave the hat on," she said again. "This entire look you have right now is hot as fuck."

I had to hold back every part that said to throw her into the pillows and fuck her like I planned on doing on that railing. "Sit this pussy on my face, princess. *Now*."

Chapter Fourteen
Des

I think I've died.

I think I've died and gone to a special Hell where your darkest desires are listed on a whiteboard, and the person of your dreams is fulfilling each, one by one.

God, the way he moved his tongue, sucked on me, slapped and grabbed my ass or my breasts, and made my body move... And he'd been living across the hall from me the entire time?

I could have been being pleasured like this for an entire year.

I was such a fucking idiot.

I grabbed the headboard and nearly limped over it, my elbows braced across the top, my teeth imprinting in the wood. Shit, I was going to scream.

His hat fell off mere moments after he'd started in on me, and I picked it up and placed it front ways on my head. I didn't know how I was going to come again, but with every lick down my center, every slip of his tongue inside me, and the way he was slapping my ass, I pained at the feeling of another orgasm rising. He blew against me, nibbled on my clit, and sucked it into his mouth. The delicious sensations made me limp. I could barely hold myself up, and I was scared that he wouldn't be able to breathe if I didn't.

But after a few more seconds, I forgot about allowing him to breathe. I rocked on his tongue as he held me tight. I bit that fucking headboard until my teeth marks were left behind, and then I came—*hard*, almost embarrassingly—on his tongue.

I fell back against the sheet as my orgasm wafted through me, willing my breaths to even and my heart to stop throbbing. Eyes closed, I counted my shallow breaths and nearly fell asleep again. Though the bed shifted after a few seconds, and I felt his body atop mine.

"How fucking sexy are you in my hat," he grunted before kissing my breast.

I smiled broadly, my body curling up as I pulled his head off my nipple. "I don't think you're getting anything else out of me," I told him.

Axel looked behind me at the clock on the wall. "It's just minutes to sunrise, princess," he said. "I still plan on fucking you while that equinox sun rises."

I reached for his hat and put it back on his head. "Then you'll need this," I said. "And I'll need water and a massage."

He pushed a stray hair off my face and kissed my lips, prompting another moan from me.

That smirking smile stared at me when he pulled back. "Hang tight."

I watched him through hazy eyes as he stretched into the kitchen and returned with a glass of water and a banana. I didn't hesitate when he sat on the bed and gave them to me. He chuckled under his breath as I practically inhaled both.

"Mmm… I think this is the best banana I've ever had," I said as I laid back on the pillow and savored the taste in my mouth.

"I'll get us actual breakfast in a bit," he said.

I tossed the banana peel in the trash and swished the water in my mouth before lying down again. A heavy sigh left me as I looked him over, the first peek of sunlight pushing its way through my window.

I wondered if I looked as satiated as he did.

"Do you know what I want?" I asked. A breeze circled the room from the open window, billowing my sheer white curtains, and Axel laid down at my side, scooting closer until he could wrap his arms around my waist. The look in his eyes was soft, dilated, content, and maybe even…

Maybe even happy.

"What's that?" he asked.

"I want a lifetime," I whispered, my nails grazing his cheek. His fingers kneaded my waist, and I drowned in his darkened gaze. I knew it was a risk even saying it since we'd just spent our first night together, but something about it felt more right than anything I'd felt before.

I'd been swept off my feet—quite literally, too. I had those butterflies. I had that melted heart. I was sure if he left me to go back to his apartment, I'd be checking my phone every few minutes for a message from him.

I was in deeper than I'd ever been, and I was loving every minute.

"What do you want?" I asked him.

"Everything that you'll give me," he said, making those butterflies in my stomach flutter again. He pushed my hair back and gave my chin a gentle flick that made me smile. "Under one condition."

"What's that?"

"You tell anyone about the pumpkin spice, and you'll not be able to walk for a week."

My grin widened. "Your threats sound like too much fun," I said.

He grabbed my ass and slid me flush, eliciting another moan from deep within. The dig of his fingers in my flesh made me wince and throb in the best way. And when he leaned forward to lick the column of my throat, my will collapsed.

I sighed in his arms as he muttered, "Everything, princess," against my skin. "I want everything with you, starting with this first sunrise."

Chapter Fifteen
Axel

My stomach and heart were a fluttering disaster after what we'd just said to each other. But I meant it. I did want everything with her. I wanted to try it, wanted to try *this*.

I picked her up on my waist and carried her outside onto her balcony, where, unlike at my apartment, she could watch the sun come up.

Every tree in the city was in the midst of changing colors. The golden sun blanketed every corner of every building around us, the trees reflecting off the mirrored glass.

"Every equinox, my mother would tell us to look at the sunrise and think of all the things we've left behind in the last year," I told her. "She told us to celebrate this morning with intentions and gratitude, to look at the future with want." I looked down at Des and pushed her hair back. "I never knew what that meant until tonight."

"So, it's not just a sunrise fetish?" she teased me.

I smiled at her. "It's not." I kissed her nose and snaked my hands around her waist. "You are the thing I'm grateful for. This new life with you."

"I like that," she said, and she wrapped her arms around my neck and kissed me deeply before I could say anything more.

Being naked on the balcony with her, the cool autumn

breeze around us, and the sun basking on our bodies... this was my favorite morning ever.

I twisted her around and pinned her between myself and the rail, my fingers taking note of her body again, massaging her breasts and hips, letting her sink onto my chest. My cock stiffened at her feel, and I was sure I would never tire of that.

"Grab the railing and arch your back for me," I whispered in her ear.

She clasped onto the iron rail and shifted to open up for me: arching her back so beautifully, her toes curling in anticipation. The slight wiggle of her ass made my hand crease on her hips as I stepped back and pumped my cock a few times at the sight of her enticing body, the view of that glistening pussy spreading for me.

I tapped my dick on her ass and teased at her entrance with the tip, eliciting a whimper from her that made me groan her name. Fuck, she was swollen. Swollen from me. From how much I'd taken from her that night. My cock throbbed at the thought as I took more of her. The fit... God, she fit perfectly around me.

"Look at that sunrise, baby," I finally said. "Memorize every ray of sunlight and shadow cast over this little town. Memorize it as the first of so many more you'll wake to my cock sliding in and out of you."

"Fuck, Axel," she moaned. Her body limped as she groaned, and she leaned over the railing as if she were giving out.

I kissed her bare spine before wrapping my hands around her breasts, making her body arch upward again as I gathered a pace. I pumped deliberately in and out of her, relishing the noise of her wetness around me.

The slight noise of surrender that left her spoke to the deepest part of my soul. I grabbed her left arm and secured it behind her back as she lifted her bent leg to the rail, letting me deeper inside her. Shit, I could have continued that tease for hours, *days*. But I could feel her beginning to collapse around me, her legs trembling with the release that would make her pass out completely.

"You're doing so well, baby," I told her. "So fucking well. Do you want my cum in that swollen pussy, Des?"

"Yes—shit—*yes*," she pleaded, her eyes shut. "God, I'm going to—"

"One more time, princess," I begged. "One more."

A high-pitched whimper came from her as I took her hair in my hand, exposing her neck with a gentle tug.

"Fuck yes, Axel, right there—" I cursed the air at how much wetter she became with the tug on her hair. Her whimpers became more urgent with every move. Shit, her pussy was tightening so much around me. I watched as her mouth opened, and she tried to swallow a scream as her cunt pulsed over my dick. Any words from her lips turned to mutters. She fought her collapse, but I needed her to give in to it.

I pulled her up and pinned her arms around my neck, my fingers circling her waist to her clit. Her knees weakened.

"Let go, baby," I whispered as I pressed her swollen clit. "Give me what's mine."

Her gasp was a prayer. Her body shuddered. She limped and whimpered and squirmed. And as she screamed and came apart around me, I lost control of my own body, too.

Together, we came. Our bodies were a perfect unison of pleasure. Her knees almost gave out, but she held tight to my arms as she regained breath.

I stared at the sunrise, pure satisfaction swelling over my muscles and seeping into my bones as we came down together. When I pulled out of her, I turned her around and grasped her beneath her ass. She surrendered in my arms, her legs spread over my waist as I sat us down in the chair she had on her balcony.

Her cheek leaned into my hand, and I pushed her hair back so I could admire the sunlight brightening her brown eyes. They almost looked like honey in this light. She was so fucking gorgeous that it hurt.

"I think this is the best blind date I've ever been on," she muttered, and I could hear the smile in her voice.

"Maybe one day I'll take you on a different kind of blind date," I said.

"Mm…" She shifted on my lap and wrapped her arms around my neck. "So many dirty promises, Axel Connors. How am I supposed to pace myself?"

I squeezed her ass and started to caress up and down her side. "A lifetime, princess," I said before kissing her. "We have a lifetime."

Epilogue
Des

The turbulence on the small prop plane had me nervous.

It jolted hard against the wind, and Axel grabbed my hand on the rest. I chuckled as I turned to see his eyes shut tight, his jaw taut.

"Shut up," he grumbled. "Don't you need to clutch a crystal? Count your breaths?"

The sight of how hot he was in his baseball cap and snug shirt, nervous from a bit of turbulence, made me bite my lip. "Watching you squirm is keeping my mind off of it," I retaliated. "What happened to the tough guy act? Mr. I-never-get-sick."

"Not sick—" he made a grunting noise, obviously trying to relax at the next bump. "Why are we going here again?"

"It's your family," I said. "You haven't seen them in two years."

"Should have taken the boat," he muttered.

I took my hand from beneath his and reached into his lap, slowly massaging his inner thigh. "Want me to keep you distracted?" I asked.

One brow raised, his eye peeked open at me. He clenched the armrests again with another jolt but didn't push me off. "I'm listening," he said.

The captain's voice came over the intercom, announcing

that we would be out of the turbulence in the next few minutes.

A deep breath came from him, making my smile widen. I relaxed my head against the rest once more, abandoning the mile-high tease I'd started—and just in time. The plane jolted again, and my stomach twisted.

"If we die during landing, I love you," Axel said without opening his eyes.

"I love you," I said. "But if something happens, I'll drag us out and annoy you until you come back to life."

His thumb caressed the top of my hand, his lip flinching like he might smile. "I'll make sure to take a nap in the afterlife first. Make you sweat a bit."

We were heading to the small town in Alaska where his family lived, and next week... next week, we were going to elope on the coast of Washington.

The last two years with him had been more amazing than any other years of my life.

Axel took on a traveling job with a company building luxury treehouses about eighteen months ago. We sold all of our things and bought a van, and I took my photography business on the road with us. Getting to see and photograph the rest of the country had been my ultimate dream, and I was living it. *We* were living our dreams together.

Of course, we were sure Koko loved it more than the both of us combined.

I didn't know where life would take us next, but as I squeezed his hand again and looked sideways at the rugged man at my side, I knew nothing would tear us apart.

"As long as you come back to me," I said.

He brought my hand to his lips and gave me a reassuring smile. "Always."

The End.

THANK YOU
for reading

Anyone And You
An Autumn erotica novella

If you enjoyed this story, please
consider leaving a review on
Amazon, Goodreads, social media
sites, or your preferred review site.
Reviews really mean a lot (even if it
us just a couple lines) and help us as
authors get our stories out there.

Acknowledgments

I know in the past I've said this was going to be short, but this one really is.

To my ravens, thank you all SO SO much for continuing to support my wild ideas and shenanigans through this journey. You all are the absolute best team I could have, and I cannot thank you enough.

To Kay, thank you for bringing Mr. Grumpy Lumberjack into my life, and thank you for not looking at me like I was crazy when I decided to combine it with my want for a carnival novella. You the best!

To Emily, I can't thank you enough for helping me through the editing process with this one! You did amazing. I'm so proud of you, and I can't wait to see where this takes you.

To Lex, thank you for always helping me out with beta reads and hyping me up! I am so excited to read your fall novellas and all the things you do.

To all the ARC readers, thank you so much for continuing to be awesome and spreading the word about my little works. It always amazes me how much reach you all have, and I appreciate you SO MUCH. I couldn't do this without you. Thank you, thank you, thank you!

To my family, thank you for always helping me out and supporting me. I wouldn't be able to take time to write these without your help and keeping me sane. I love y'all.

And to my readers… Thank you! I don't know how else to thank you except to continue to give you everything I have and to bring more and more to the table to give back to you all. Thank you for being patient with me and sharing and reviewing.

See you all next month for the Bloody Mary novella.

Other Works by Jack Whitney

Now Available:

Dead Moons Rising
Book One in the Honest Scrolls Series

Flames of Promise
Book Two in the Honest Scrolls Series

The Gathering
An Honest Scrolls Novella

Sweet Girl
A Cupid Novella

Ballad of Nightmares
Book One in the Nightmares Duology

Anyone And You
An autumn erotica novella

Coming Soon in 2022:

Break The Glass
A Halloween erotica novella
October 2022

Title T.B.D.
A Jack Frost Novella
December 6th, 2022

About The Author

Jack Whitney is an adult dark fantasy and romance author
out of North Carolina, US.
You can usually find her playing in dark and strange worlds.
Her characters are always in charge.
She is fueled by coffee, whiskey, and shadow daydreams. If
you're reading her books, they probably came with a
warning label.

Welcome to the Nightmare of Ravens.

Jack also feels very weird about writing bios because she's
not sure what you want to know.
She is almost always stalking social media and
procrastinating, so if you would like to find her to ask more
questions, please feel free.
@Jack.Whitney.Writer